EEEEE-Mail!

Digital 8 Sally Odgers

Illustrated by David Pearson

2000 Barrie Publishing Pty Limited
EEEEE-Mail!
Text copyright © Sally Odgers
Illustrations copyright © David Pearson

Momentum program © Barrie Publishing Pty Limited

Published by Troll Communications L.L.C.
Reprinted by arrangement with Barrie Publishing Pty Limited,
89 High Street, Kew, Australia, 3101

ISBN 0 8167 6826 9

Prepress by Splitting Image Colour Studio Pty Ltd
Printed in Singapore by PH Productions Pte Ltd
10 9 8 7 6 5 4 3 2 1

Contents Digital 8

4

Chapter One

Cyber-spook

The banshee is going to find me. I know that, and it doesn't please me one little bit.

Some dogs have fleas. Some kids have zits. Some Irish families have banshees. You can get rid of the fleas with a flea collar. If you're desperate, you can try a squirt of insect repellent.

You can get rid of zits with stuff from the drugstore or—again if you're really desperate—by changing your diet and drinking lots of water.

The books and stores are full of stuff you can use for getting rid of unwelcome visitors, but there's not a single word about banshees.

I know. I've been through three libraries, eleven encyclopedias, nine volumes of *Weird Tales,* and fifteen horror writers. One place I haven't checked is the Internet. How can I? It was the Internet that caused all the trouble!

My name, by the way, is Kathleen O'Grady. I have red hair and green eyes. Yes, I admit I sound just like a stereotype, but that's not my fault. Blame the O'Grady genes for the looks, and my parents for my name.

A minute ago I said it was the Internet that caused all the trouble. That isn't really true, of course. The Internet is just millions of files in computers, all linked up around the world. People put words and pictures and music onto the Internet so that other people can share them. Some of the stuff isn't very nice, but nobody forces you to look or listen to that. Look at it this way: the television has an on/off switch and your Internet browser has that little icon up in the top right-hand corner.

Click! and you're out of the site.

That's what usually happens, anyway. Except when it comes to the banshee.

Now, I use the Internet at school, of course, but I never have enough time to look up all the cool stuff I want to see. So when Dad got our home PC connected, I dived right in and began to surf. It was Halloween, the day we got connected.

Big mistake, but we didn't know that then.

Well, first of all I looked for some chat rooms. I wanted to chat with people in other countries. I guess I signed in and out of about fifteen of them before I realized that they weren't really what I was looking for. They were full of people trying to sound cool.

After a while, I gave up chatting and played online games instead. I played with an Irish girl who wanted to play online chess, and a computer whiz who also lived in Ireland. Oh, and there was even an Irish prince!

It was after one of the chess games (the Irish girl won) that an e-mail popped up on our server.

"EEEEEEEEE! Woe to the House of O'Grady."

That's what it said.

Oh, no, I thought. We've got a cyber-spook. That's what I thought—really—but at first I didn't know how right I was!

You see, spooks are what Dad calls those people who make nuisances of themselves on the Internet. They leave threatening or stupid e-mails on your server and say horrible things in the chat rooms. Some of them even try to send you viruses that will infect your computer.

It's easy to get away from most of these cyber-spooks. You just delete their e-mails and refuse to accept any files or chat requests they try to send. Oh, and you can click away from them in the chat rooms. The thing you mustn't do is to give them your real name or any other information they can use to track you down. You have to give your real name and e-mail address to the hosts of the chat rooms, but they're not supposed to give it out to anyone else.

Dad had told me these things thirty million times before he let me use the computer, and I did what he said. For real!

Sometimes it was difficult, like when my Irish chess friend wanted to send me a genuine gold-plated shamrock from Ireland.

Then there was the time my computer-whiz friend wanted to send me a pre-release game about leprechauns.

There was also the time my royal friend wanted to send me a silver Celtic cross as a present.

I'd have loved to get these presents, but my friends couldn't send them to me. Not unless I gave out my real name and address. Dad had been very, very definite that I was never to do that.

So... how had this cyber-spook found out my real name?

Chapter Two

A Serious Cyber-mistake

'EEEEEEEEE! Woe to Kathleen, last of the House of O'Grady.'

I sat staring at the horrible e-mail message. I thought I must have let something slip, sometime, to someone.

If Dad found out about this, he'd probably ban me from using the computer. So I did the obvious thing. I clicked Delete and sent the cyber-spook's e-mail message to the recycle bin. Then I emptied the recycle bin, just to make sure it was really gone.

After that, I didn't feel like surfing the Internet, so I disconnected, turned off the computer, and went to play softball with my friends in the park.

The next day it was raining, so I turned on the computer to do some surfing. I clicked the little Mail icon to see if we had any e-mail. And there it was. Another e-mail from the cyber-spook.

"EEEEEEEEE! Woe to Kathleen, last of the House of O'Grady."

My stomach did a funny sort of dip and bounce, then I calmed down. I started to wonder if it might be Dad, trying to be funny. (Yes, you can send e-mail to your own address. It's really easy.)

I deleted the e-mail and turned off the computer.

Later on that day, I mentioned the House of O'Grady, in a sort of roundabout way, to Dad.

"There's the House of Lords and the House of Commons in England, and the House of Hair and the House of Beauty," I said. "I wonder if there's a House of O'Grady somewhere?"

Dad stared at me suspiciously.

"Wouldn't it be weird if there were?" I said.

"Have you been talking to Grandpa?" asked Dad, and his voice was as suspicious as his face.

"Not lately," I said. "Why?"

"That 'House of O'Grady' thing sounds like something he'd come up with. If you're interested in making lists of 'Houses' you might add 'The House of Horrors.' That's in a wax museum somewhere. Then there's 'The House of Usher.' I think that was the title of an old book."

I decided it wasn't Dad who was sending the e-mail after all.

The next day I connected to the Internet and there was another message waiting on the server.

"EEEEEEEE! Woe to flame-haired Kathleen, last of the House of O'Grady."

By now, I was getting really annoyed with the cyber-spook. I was also getting really worried, because I knew it was only a matter of time before Dad saw one of the messages.

I knew for sure I'd never told anyone on the Internet the color of my hair. I hadn't sent anyone a photograph of myself, either. This was getting really weird, so I clicked on the Reply button and sent a message back to the cyber-spook.

"Get lost."

I clicked on Send. As soon as the message had vanished from the screen, I knew I'd made a serious cyber-mistake. I'd established a dialogue with the cyber-spook, and now he—she? it?—would be encouraged to keep on pestering me.

Chapter Three

Cyber-screams

I was right to be worried. As soon as I'd told the cyber-spook to get lost, the little Mail icon lit up on the toolbar. I was tempted to recycle it straight away, but I had the sudden idea it might be one of my cyber-friends playing a knock-knock joke. Only with cyber-screams instead of the knocks.

I held my breath and crossed my fingers and clicked on the little icon.

"EEEEEEEEE! Woe to the flame-haired, green-eyed Kathleen, last of the House of O'Grady."

I was about to recycle this message, but this time, I kept my head. I checked the return address:

Banshee@wraithnet.co.uk

"Get lost, cyber-spook," I typed, and hit Send.

Instantly, the icon lit up again with another cyber-scream.

"EEEEEEEEE! Woe to the flame-haired, green-eyed Kathleen, last of the House of O'Grady." The address was: www.bansheechat/hi/earlywarning.co.uk.

Okay, so I should have left it at that, but by now I was getting interested. This cyber-spook was inviting me to a chat room so we could have a real dialogue.

It couldn't do any harm to find out what he/she/it wanted, I thought, so I went straight to that address. I gave my particulars to the chat room host (you have to do that, remember, otherwise you're not allowed to use the chat rooms) and then I went inside.

The cyber-spook was already online, so we established a dialogue. Did we ever! It went like this.

Banshee: EEEEEEEEE!

Kathleen: Well? What do you want?

Banshee: EEEEEEEEE!

Kathleen: Yes, I heard you. What do you want?

Banshee: Gotcha!

Kathleen: Is this some kind of joke?

Banshee: No joke, sister. EEEEEEEEE! Woe to the flame-haired, green-eyed Kathleen, last of the House of O'Grady. Your doom is sealed.

Kathleen: Who are you? What are you talking about?

Banshee: I am the hereditary banshee of the House of O'Grady. Download me now for maximum effect. You never know when you might need an early-warning system!

I got out of that chat room, fast. I clicked on all the little X buttons, then I clicked on Home.

The screen flickered, the address changed, and there it was again: www.bansheechat/hi/earlywarning. co.uk.

Banshee: EEEEEEEEE!

I didn't say anything that time. I just clicked Home.

The screen flickered, the address changed, and there it was again: www.bansheechat/hi/earlywarning. co.uk.

I disconnected from the Internet and turned off the computer. My hands were shaking, and my stomach was bouncing around like a rodeo horse. I counted up to sixty, slowly. Then I crossed my fingers and switched the computer back on.

The icons flashed, passwords typed themselves, the Internet connected, and there it was again: www.banshee chat/hi/earlywarning.co.uk.

You know what I did then? I did what I should have done in the first place. I turned off the computer and went to find Dad.

Chapter Four

BANSHEEEEEEE!

Dad was writing up his automobile log book when I found him. He was adding up miles on a calculator and multiplying them by units of money.

"What is it, Kathleen?" he asked, peering at me over the glasses he uses for accounting. "Is something the matter?"

"There's a cyber-spook in a chat room on the computer," I said.

"Well, that's easily solved. Get out of the chat room," said Dad, reasonably. "Click on the little X."

"I've tried that. It won't go away."

Dad sighed. "Disconnect and switch off then."

"I tried that, too. It keeps coming back to that address. It says it's a banshee."

Dad's gaze had been straying back toward his calculator, but when I said that, he snapped to attention. "I'd better come and have a look," he said.

Dad came into the living room and turned on the computer. It went into its warm-up routine. Then, without even completing its system check, it connected itself to the Internet. Up popped www.bansheechat/hi/earlywarning.co.uk.

"EEEEEEEEE!" said the banshee.

"Get lost," typed Dad.

"Greetings, Dermot O'Grady. I am the hereditary banshee of the House of O'Grady. Download me now for maximum effect. You never know when you might need an early-warning system!"

Dad gulped. He even went pale. "Oh, no," he said. "Oh, my goodness!"

"What is it?" I gasped. "Is it a terrible cyber-virus or something?"

"Apparently it is now," said Dad. "It's mutated!" He put his hands over his face and groaned, softly. "I'd heard the wretched things were keeping up with the times," he said, "but I had no idea it could track us here through the Internet."

"I haven't downloaded anything," I said. "I promise I haven't."

Dad wasn't listening to me. He was muttering under his breath.

"What is this cyber-spook?" I yelled. "Talk to me, Dad!"

Dad jumped. "This cyber-spook, as you call it, is really a banshee," he said flatly.

"I know that. It just told us. What I want to know is, what's a banshee?"

Dad gave me a harried look. "A banshee is an Irish spook, Kathleen. It has the head of a rabbit and the body of a woman, and it wears a tattered shroud."

"Oh," I said. "That sounds pretty weird."

"Banshees," said Dad, "commonly haunt Irish castles. They prowl the battlements of their chosen castles by night, and they scream whenever they think someone's going to die."

"I see," I said. "And what about this banshee of the House of O'Grady?"

Chapter Five

Your Host, The Banshee of the O'Gradys

Dad gave another groan. A really hollow one this time.

"The banshee of the House of O'Grady is the reason your great-grandfather left Ireland," he said. "You see, Kathleen, it kept on screaming, night after night, whenever so much as a sparrow was due to fall off a tree. Your great-grandfather could never get any sleep. All the servants left, and he was all alone. He tried to sell the castle, but no one would buy it, so in the end he did a moonlight flit."

"What's that?"

"A moonlight flit? That means he left home very suddenly without any warning. He went off to visit a neighbor one night, and instead of going home, he stowed away on a ship."

I might have laughed at the idea of my great-grandfather sneaking off like that, but Dad was deadly serious.

"Your great-grandfather left his friends and relatives, and he deliberately lost contact with everyone he knew, so the banshee wouldn't know where he was."

"Did it work?" I asked.

"Yes," said Dad. "It worked until now. Now the thing's tracked us down."

"It doesn't know anything more than our e-mail address and our names," I said.

"That's bad enough," said Dad. "Now that it's on the Internet, it can check bank account numbers and electoral rolls and tax files. It'll find us, sooner or later, you'll see."

"I haven't told anyone my name though," I protested. "I promise I haven't! So how did the thing know who I was?"

"You told no one?" said Dad, suspicious.

"No one! Not even the Irish prince and the computer expert and the chess girl!"

"Who on earth are they?" asked Dad.

I told Dad all about them, and about the wonderful gifts they wanted to send me. "I really wanted those presents, too," I said, "but I did what you said and didn't give them my name and address."

"They sound like hoaxes to me," said Dad grimly. "The wretched banshee's been masquerading as these cyber-friends of yours to try and get our address. If you'd accepted any of those gifts, Kathleen, you would have had more than you bargained for!" He frowned. "Are you sure you've never given your name online? Not for any reason?"

"Well ... only to the hosts of the chat rooms," I said. "You have to do that or they won't let you in. They don't tell anyone else who you are, though."

"Not usually, no," agreed Dad. He stared at the address that was still on-screen: www.bansheechat/hi/earlywarning.co.uk.

"Banshee chat," said Dad, after a few moments. "I might have guessed. That's a banshee chat room and the darned thing is the host." He laughed, bitterly. "Your host, the Banshee of the House of O'Grady! It sounds like a television game show. It must have been hosting one of the chat rooms you entered."

Well, what could we do? What would you have done? We disconnected the computer from the Internet. Permanently. But Dad says it won't do more than buy us some time. Dad says he's quite sure the Banshee of the House of O'Grady is going through all the cyber-records that it can find, and eventually it will find us. It will find out where we live. Any day now, it could plop through the mailbox in an airmail package. It could show up at the front door.

Meanwhile, we never open mail if we don't know where it comes from, and we're searching everywhere we can think of for a way to get rid of the thing when it does arrive. So far, Dad's read twenty-four volumes of Celtic mythology, and I've been through three libraries, eleven encyclopedias, nine volumes of *Weird Tales,* and fifteen horror writers. One place we haven't checked is the Internet, and now you know why.

Has anyone got any suggestions?